# THE MAGICAL BICYCLE

*To Tim*
B.D.

*To Archie*
C.B.

First published in Picture Lions in 1996
3 5 7 9 10 8 6 4 2
Picture Lions is an imprint of the Children's Division,
part of HarperCollins Publishers Ltd,
77-85 Fulham Palace Road, Hammersmith, London W6 8JB
First published in Great Britain by
HarperCollins Publishers Ltd in 1995
Text copyright © Berlie Doherty 1995
Illustrations copyright © Christian Birmingham 1995
The author and illustrator assert the moral right to be
identified as the author and illustrator of the work.
A CIP catalogue for this title is
available from the British Library.
ISBN: 0 00 664614 X
Printed and bound in Italy

# THE MAGICAL BICYCLE

Berlie Doherty

Illustrated by Christian Birmingham

PictureLions

*An Imprint of HarperCollinsPublishers*

My best surprise
Was my shining bike
With its silver voice
But I couldn't ride it.

Every time I tried it
Threw me off.
I think it thought
It was a horse.

I bruised my knees.
I banged my chin.

My brother can glide it
Round and round.
Jenny can race it up and down
Even my uncle can wobble astride it
Everybody I know can ride it.

It must be something to do with magic.
There must be a special, secret trick.
There must be a spell on bikes, I decided.

Dad ran up the entry, holding on,
And then he ran all the way down
And panted all the way up again.

"Just turn your legs!"
He grew tired and slow,
"You won't fall off..."

And I never did
Till he let go.

But every night, deep in my dreams
I rode my bike
Over the trees,
As high as the birds,
Over the mountains
Over the world.

And every day I tried again.
I gave my dad another chance
"I WILL ride my bike!" I shouted out loud.

And I fell off.

I spat on my hands
And rubbed my knees
I picked up my bike
And tried to look proud.

"It's just a matter of magic," I said.
"That's all it is."

And then one day,
I must have
Said it.
The magic word.
I didn't hear it.
I didn't think it.
It must have been
Deep in the quietest bit of my mind.

There was Dad, running behind me,
I could hear his footsteps
Fainter and fainter,
I could feel the air
On my face and my hair
I could feel my own power
I could feel my own strength
I could hear the wheels turning.
My legs were like pistons
And I knew I could do it
I could cycle for ever.

Like a bird over mountains
Like a ship over oceans
To the end of the world
I had magic in me.